D1707391

Kilroy's Necropolis, Circle 2:

The Raptor's Games

Anony Mou5

Dedicated to Nessa Eichorn.

INTRODUCTION

I wrote this book for adults. It's full of adult shit, adult words, world issues, all that. It's explicit content. That said: Welcome to all the kids reading this. If you're looking for a book that isn't some weak ass shit, you've found it.

I acknowledge the older kids who can handle what's in this book. I also know some adults can't take this book. Can you?

I was in middle school when I read "Of Mice and Men" by Steinbeck. The honest portrayal of brutality with innocence taught me something. Not everything is right in the world. Too much is wrong.

I hope this book will be such for someone else. You might need to take care of yourself or your siblings at home. You don't want condescending bullshit about what you can't handle.

Sometimes adults don't want to talk about something. You very well could have the weight of protecting yourself on your growing shoulders. This was me.

If you are like I was then, these books are for you now.

You kids are coming for us one day.

PREFACE

This book is formatted for easy readability and has dyslexic readers in mind.

BIRTH

Kilroy didn't want to be awake. Da Vinci was in her doorway, preventing sleep.

"Rise and Shine, Kilroy! I have something amazing to show you!" he said with dazzled eyes.

"Wait, can I get dressed first?" said Kilroy as she slid her cargo pants on over her boyshorts.

"Whatever. Come on." Said Da Vinci as he turned away. Kilroy took off her shirt to put a bra on then put her shirt back on. She grabbed her gun but left her jacket.

"You don't need that where we're going. You'll see why." Said Da Vinci, pointing to her gun hanging from her shoulder while she put her mask on. She didn't usually need the mask on the ship except by the Smoking room, restaurants, and Breakfast Saloon. The vessel is as new.

Kilroy set her gun down.

"Ok."

"Follow me!" Da Vinci proclaimed with gusto. He guided Kilroy up to the boat deck near where Human Excavation met at dispatch, but amidships. He opened the gymnasium door that had been locked before.

Kilroy couldn't believe her eyes.

She was in a gymnasium that was finer made than anything she'd imagined, having grown up with modern gyms and health clubs. Her ballet studio wasn't even this ornate, not even the recital stage.

There were pillars. All the antique workout equipment was piled between the pillars and the wall.

There, filling the room, was a massive tank, like a ship in a bottle. It was painted in bright colors like the

HHumvee but with scenes from Greek mythology.

She could see a scene of a young girl being sacrificed and Trojan soldiers. She walked around and saw a scene with a woman stabbing a man trapped in a net. Then the same woman is shown upon a throne.

"It's based on the M1 Abrams, but wider and with 4 thinner tracks, a bigger gun with two smaller guns on either side on turrets mounted on top of a cockpit. There's a windshield so I can drive it like a car."

"Why do you need these guns?" Kilroy asked.

"What if someone raises an army and tries to take over Necropolis again?" Da Vinci asked Kilroy seriously.

"For real?"

"Yes. He was dealt with and banished to the library of ages. Also, guns are fun! This baby also has much more power than the Abrams. There's no need for a fuel tank, so I used that space for more engine!"

"Banished to the what?"

"It was a bitch and a half getting the shock collar on him, but if he goes beyond a specific parameter, he is in massive pain. It's a real motherfucker of a collar. Enough to stop him for now.

'Back to the tank. She's a beaut. She as vexed me. Tested me in more ways than one. I gave her the name of a never conquered woman who was assassinated like a man. Clytemnestra!" Da Vince broke a bottle of 1998 Veuve Clicquot La Grande Dame on the side of Clytemnestra. "Your mission, should you choose to accept it, is to help me get her out of the Gymnasium."

"How?"

"That's the fun part. Get in, loser." Da Vinci said as he reached for the heavy door handle. The door opened with a hiss.

Kilroy walked around to the passenger side, ducking under the cannon. She tried to open her door but without success. She knocked on the window. Da Vinci nodded his head and reached for the unlock switch. Kilroy took his nod to mean she should pull on the door handle again. The two actions canceled each other. She tried again.

"Stop. Stop." Mouthed Da Vinci as he held his hand in a halt position. He hit the switch. She heard a click. She opened the door and got in.

"Rock and roll." Said Kilroy.

"Fasten your seatbelt." Said Da Vinci as he pressed play on his phone. "The Dark Memories" by Heavenly came blasting all around her. "Grab the controller in front of you."

Kilroy looked down and saw a game controller on a stand. She picked it up and tried the right joystick. She heard the turret respond, and the screen on the dashboard lit up with footage from two cameras. One was at the base of each gun turret. She moved the left joystick, and the left turret responded.

"How do I fire?"

"L and R. One for a short burst and Two for continuous spray."

Kilroy hit L1. A short burst penetrated the wall of the gymnasium. She aimed the turrets dead center in front of the cannon. She hit L2 and R2 and moved the guns down slowly, drilling down the wall with bullets.

"Thank you. Now for the wow." Said Da Vinci as he pulled a crank to physically load the cannon. He hit the big red button. A massive depleted-uranium bullet blew the wall open. Da Vinci used his controller to drive the tank forward through the ragged wall like a cervix.

He gained speed through the wrecked promenade. They rolled down and off the bridge deck, flying out of the Titanic into the waiting sands.

Da Vinci kept driving and picked up speed. Kilroy watched the speedometer gradually reach 120 kph. She then noticed the smell of meat and blood. Kilroy looked behind the seats. She saw buckets of meat.

"Are we having a barbecue?" she asked.

"You'll see." Da Vinci replied as he slowed down and proceeded to drive around. His driving seemed aimless until Kilroy realized he was looking for something.

After a while, Clytemnestra rolled to a stop. Kilroy saw what looked like emus at first. Then she saw the feathered tails and thought they were peacocks. Then she saw them run in formation toward the tank. She saw massive claws on their feet and their tiny wings in front. Some were brightly colored, while others were tawny brown.

"HOLYSHIT!" Kilroy shouted.

"Calm down."

"What are they?"

"Utahraptor Ostrommaysi. They're dinosaurs." Da Vinci said as he grabbed a bucket of meat. Kilroy grabbed a bucket, too. She looked back out at the dino-saurs and saw that each one had a saddle on her back. Kilroy was stoked.

She opened her door and began dumping handfuls of raw meat to the joyful creatures.

"Don't give it all away. You want some left to feed them after we ride."

Kilroy saw she had about half her meat left. She looked up and was face-to-mouth with the magnificent, feathered raptor, aware she could easily bite her head clean off.

"They're ambush hunters. They attack prey larger than themselves mostly, much like humans do. You need not worry much. But they'll fuss over you like a baby if you're not careful."

Kilroy regarded the creatures and lifted one tentative hand to stroke her nose like a horse. Her nose followed Kilroy's hand as if looking for pets. It was the meat on

Kilroy's hands that had her interested.

Kilroy saw that the most dominant member of the murder was front and center. She picked up a big piece of meat and looked to see one of them cowering back and behind. She threw that one the beef. The other raptors scolded her for it.

That raptor stepped forward. Kilroy put the rest of the meat back in the tank and approached the low-status raptor. She went to the raptor's side and put her foot in the holster. She tried to step up. It was not like mounting her childhood horse. The raptor shifted her weight, making it more difficult. She grabbed the knob on the front of the saddle and pulled herself up. She swung her leg over awkwardly.

She looked down at the happy cherub faces on the saddles of the raptors. She looked and saw Da Vinci had chosen a mount and was waiting.

"I'm ready. "she said.

"Excellent. Kick her sides to direct her. Left for left and right for right. Kick both sides to start running and to stop running." Instructed Da Vinci.

"Got it." Kilroy tried it out and led the raptor in a meandering path.

"Send her this way." Da Vinci said. Kilroy complied to the best of her abilities. "If you dig your heels steadily into her sides, she'll accelerate." Kilroy did so, and soon they were all running together over the dunes and through the sands. It was glorious.

"The murder of raptors swerved to the left, and Kilroy tried to direct hers to go with them, but she turned too far. She began to run away from the murder at a right angle. Kilroy wanted to turn her around, but the raptor merely swerved. She tried to get her to stop, but she sped up.

Soon, Da Vinci and the murder were out of sight and earshot. Kilroy finally got her mount to slow to a stop.

She was freaking out internally. She saw what the sands did to the flesh.

"Ok, Mars. Think." She took a deep breath. She could smell her sweat and the warm scent of dinosaur. "That's it!"

She took off her mask and gave the air a sniff. She could smell hot metal and motor oil. She directed the raptor carefully toward that smell. She gave all of her focus. Soon she was running up over the dunes by the tank. She could see Da Vinci and the rest of the murder hurrying back over the dunes toward them.

She waved.

KISS THE BABIES

Kilroy watched the children as they approached Donde. They had a phone to sell. Donde turned the screen on and off a few times until he watched the phone's owner unlock it.

He then pulled out a laptop and booted a diagnostic program from a USB. He went to the phone app on the phone and typed in "*#0*#0" to access a hidden diagnostic menu. He looked through the information.

He exited the menu and keyed in "*#*#4636#*#*" to view usage information. He made Obama's "Not bad" face.

He plugged the phone into his laptop and used the booted diagnostic tools there as well. He then turned back toward the children.

"This phone is excellent. I'll give you this twenty-gram ingot of high karat gold." He said as he bent the deceptively heavy ingot to demonstrate his truthfulness.

The children happily took their pay and ran off to the nearest money changer to break up their prize into smaller currency units.

The phone stand was a simple glass case against one side of a long, arched corridor with beautiful tile. Behind the case was a display of purses. Goods lined every inch of reachable space, up to where the ceiling vaults.

It was the Grand Bazaar in Istanbul.

Most of the things Kilroy saw weren't for sale. The only active shops had goods dragged in and displayed in front of the shops.

Sometimes scammers work unused shops, selling the goods that are there in the Land of the Living.

Nothing can be taken from these shops perman-ently. It inevitably returns. People who have just fallen are the ones who fall for it. After that, they know better.

The Bazaar was lined with people selling things on tables and blankets, and shelves. Elaborate pop-up stores insinuated themselves into every nook and cranny.

She'd just eaten from one of the food stalls and learned the hard way not to walk from the stall with the food. She missed her chicken poppers.

The food was free. That was a big lure.

The stalls selling wares were lost in the chaos. The place was like an "I Spy" picture. That's why Kilroy was wearing a sign. It was two boards connected b. a pair of straps that went over her shoulders. The sign said, "Perfect phones! Luxury models! Aesthetic! No porn users! Unlimited Data! Minimum usage! All offers considered!"

"Want to pick some music, Mars?" asked Donde.

"System of a Down."

"Hey Google, play 'System of a Down.'"

"Chop Suey" came on through the Bluetooth speaker.

"So, Donde. Have you ever met anyone famous?" asked Kilroy with awkwardness. She wasn't great at smalltalk.

"Yeah, I have. How far back do you want me to go?"

"How about someone who died after I was born."

"And you're what? 20?"

"Yeah."

"Ok. I got into a fistfight with Fakir Musafar. I got in that pervy appropriatappropriato

"Who's Fakir Musafar?"

"He's this cat who gets credit for starting the modern primitive movement. Now, I don't know if you can tell, but I'm half Neanderthal." He said, gesturing to his face and brow.

"No shit?"

"Yes. My father. I AM a primitive! I lived and died going back and forth between the Bear people in the Mountains and my mother's people in the Valley.

"I told this to Fakir, and he got this look like he smelled something bad or had a stomach virus or something. He started talking mad shit about open-mindedness and sexual liberation through bondage, and I cut him off. I said, 'Look, our Manhood rites are not whack material! I don't see you talking about returning to modern versions of primitive housing to save the environment. I don't hear you talking about ecological design and quality of life vs. sustainability and the balance between or the spiritual advance-ment behind the initiation rites you'd fetishized.

"Primitive life was about two things: survival and togetherness. I hunted mammoths with my father's clan and carried meat back for my Aunt and her children, who were as siblings."

"Why did you do one thing with your dad but something else with your mom's people?"

"It's the difference between attrition hunting and ambush hunting. There's a fine line. Fact is, I couldn't throw a long spear worth shit. The Bear people used short spears and jabbed from the rocks. That I could do."

Kilroy stood looking down at her sign.

"So what's the deal with the phones you sell? Some of these are out of date."

"Time period doesn't matter as much as you'd think. It's how the phone was used. Some phones got used long after they stopped updating or had multiple users. It makes those phones unpredictable and less functional. The same phone used only while it was current can be a great phone. You're peeking into an era."

Kilroy looked down and saw an approaching baby wearing Kiss face paint and onesie. The stone-dark skin, far from light, made the face-paint pop.

A friendly pitbull puppy ran up to the baby and began fussing over them. A man in an Armani suit ran up after the doggo. He picked the baby up. Their face-paint was smeared by doggie kisses.

"That's too bad. Somebody took the time to paint this baby's face like Peter Criss. I can only assume the other members of Kiss are around here some- where. Should we gather the Kiss babies?"

"I don't even get the joke." Said Donde.

"The Kiss babies. Making your dreams come true?" asked Kilroy, muffled by her mask. Then it hit her. She groaned at the dadness of the joke. "Kiss the babies. God damnit."

Donde laughed. The man in the Armani suit put the fussing Peter Criss baby down.

"If I may tip you, lady?" said the Armani suit man. He held a nickel in his hand.

"Five cents?" Kilroy asked, offended.

"I always have nickels in my pockets. In life, I gave away all my nickels to fellow beggars."

"I'm not a beggar."

"Take it anyway. And try dancing with your sign. You want buyers for your commission." He said as he did the cabbage patch. His dog jumped around at his feet. "She's on commission, right?" Mr. Nickels asked Donde.

"Base pay plus commission."

"Hear that? You gotta hustle! Do the hustle with me!" He did the hustle.

"O-ok." Said Kilroy awkwardly. She started to move around a little, bending at the knees.

"I used to dance to keep warm in the New York winters. Didn't work every time. I had to sleep eventually. I crashed out during a cold snap under some cardboard. Now I'm here. And I'm fucking wearing Armani!" He danced harder.

"Hey Google, play "Staying Alive" by the BeeGees."

"So chica, what's your name?"

"Kilroy."

"Nice! You ever go to school dances, Kilroy?"

"I went to a few."

"Well, you're dancing like a Public School kid right now. Dance like a maniac! School's out, baby!" shouted Mr. Nickels.

Kilroy was starting to get into it. She bobbed her head more and put her arms up over it in a ballet pose. She kicked her leg up high. She couldn't go en pointe in her combat boots, but she could leap. So she leaped. The board behind her floated up like a stiff cape and bounced back down as she landed.

"Fuck you, East Madison High! Except for Mr. Blaskoff! He was the shit!" She refused to mention the staff who took their issues out on students.

"How was he different?"

"He went to bat for me when I tried out for football. He encouraged me and talked them into it when I tried out and proved I was good enough. Quarterback right here!" she said proudly.

"They weren't going to let you?"

"Not at first, no."

"Ahoy, matey!" said an approaching voice. It was the Masked Stranger. He approached them in his customary red tracksuit.

"Oh hey! This is my shipmate." Said Kilroy politely.

"Pleased to meet you all. So, what are we talking about?" asked the Masked Stranger.

"Public school and the bullshit aspects."

"Ah yes. We don't need no education. Public schooling refuses to accommodate special minds. They fail both the best and the worst." Pontificated the Masked Stranger, killing the mood.

"I wouldn't know. I was taught by my families. I guess you could say I was a homeschool kid. It was B.S. Before Schooling. There was but one class: survive. Lessons included how to ambush mammoths and which mushrooms to eat." Said Donde.

"How old were you when you began hunting those things?" asked Mr. Nickels. His dog was lying at his feet, pooped.

"I'd seen 8 winters my first lesson." Said Donde. They were impressed.

"What's your dog's name?" queried the Masked
Stranger.

"Boomer." Replied Mr. Nickels. He watched with
unease as the Masked Stranger bent down to pet the
puppy.

"I think I did singing lessons when I was 8. At one
point, my father tried to interest me in beekeeping,
but I just wanted to draw." He said with regret.

"Yeah. I'm out." Said Mr. Nickels. He scooped up his
dog and walked briskly away.

Kilroy and Donde looked at each other, puzzled by
Mr. Nickels and his sudden departure.

"Well, that was rude. Donde, sir. You have a fascin-
ating lineage. Speaking of roots, my non-conformist
roots have come alive in Death. I was reminded of
that today, Mars. Thank you. I believe I would like to
add to your commission. What's your best deal, Mr.
Donde?"

"It's just Donde, and that would be this one I just got in. Good phone, but I shouldn't have bought it—the Tumblr activity. There's no porn usage per se, but lots of Tumblr at night. She's a lovely woman, the phone's primary user. She has a very successful aesthetic Instagram. But there are lots of pictures of women. Tasteful nudes and ludes, and many are even clothed. I don't know if I can advertise this as porn-free, is the thing. I can sell it at cost-"

"I'll take it!" he said as he took a long Harley Davidson wallet full of American bills from the inner pocket of his jacket. He offered a bundle of Benjis.

"Do these bills stay together, or did the changer bind them?" asked Donde.

"They stay together."

"Dope." Said Donde as he handed the Stranger the phone.

"Mars, may you find happiness on all of your birthdays." Said the Stranger. He handed her the phone.

ON A BOAT

Kilroy saw a cat sleeping by a wall. The cat had a glowing marble pattern that was swirling. She was twitching. Kilroy considered waking her but decided to let her lie. She walked on.

After walking a few blocks away from the Bazaar, she found who she was looking for.

"क्या आपको बाल कटवाने की आवश्यकता है?" he said.

"I'm sorry. هل تفهم اللغة العربية؟"

"حلاقة شعر."

Kilroy sat down in the tall Hollywood director's chair next to the man's cart. It was a Medieval spice wagon loaded down with hair care products. An excellent way to tell if someone is legit and not a scammer is if they have modern wares on an antique.

The man asked her how she wanted her hair. Kilroy said "High and tight" in broken Arabic. The man looked confused, then a light came to his face. He readied his clippers with oil.

Hair was falling away. It'd taken 27 Daybreaks for Da Vinci to finally get Kilroy some daywork. She wondered how long the days really were as she saw large tufts of hair fall away and play on the ground in the breeze. Her hair had grown way faster than it should in 27 days. She could pull the sides out almost three inches.

Kilroy was confused when she felt the hairdresser doing stripes on her sides and back. Soon he was finished, and he produced a mirror. She saw the misunderstanding. He'd given her a slick hi-top with vaporwave blinds on the sides.

She accepted that he gave her the wrong haircut. She also acknowledged how she liked the hair. She accepted the hair.

"‏انه جيد.‏"

"No good. Stripped." Said the hairdresser as he picked up a lock of hair from the ground and rubbed it between his fingers, showing Kilroy.

Kilroy was a little insulted. She accepted that she'd been going light on haircare since she was borrowing everything she used, though.

The man led her to his cart and began picking products for her. He showed her each one. Some had English writing and some Korean. She saw a mois-turizer, a pomade, a mask, two shampoos, a deep conditioner, and a leave-in conditioner. She smelled shea, argan oil, green tea, tea tree, essential oils, chemicals, and some fragrances.

"Use every time til gone." He said as he held up the deep conditioner. He handed her everything in a birthday gift bag.

She took some cash out of her pocket and tried to guess how much to give. She gave him 100 pounds in 10-pound notes. He put his hand to his chest and smiled. He graciously accepted 80.

There was a ring of train stations near the edge of Necropolis that were all the Copenhagen train station but from different times. Kilroy walked toward the nearest one.

She saw a small 13th century Ottoman Christian church sticking halfway out of the ground. Sand eddied around the slit windows.

She saw a group of monks next to it. Their eyes were sewn shut. They lined up before a sighted Abbot, who spoke soft Hebrew as he laid a sacramental LSD tab on the tongue of each monk. They all began to ecstatically dance. "Delirious" by Steve Aoki played from a Bluetooth speaker.

Kilroy saw a gleaming flash from her left. She turned to look. Her eyes were dazzled by an indefinite being of light. The being accepted a roll of American bills and Euros hi-fived into his clawed hand by a Kurdish man. He lo-fived an 8th of cocaine into the man's hand. The man turned to look at Kilroy.

"Ain't no thing but a chicken wing." He said with a wink. He did a bump.

Kilroy looked to see where the being of light went. She began to follow as he turned down Pall-Mall street. He yeeted onto a building and scaled up and over.

Kilroy didn't have time to figure it out. She was being approached by three young men in bathing suits. One was wearing a black speedo, one an electric blue tankini, and one a Victorian bathing suit with pale red stripes.

They all three looked at her with excitement. She looked back to the building the being had spidered up.

"How are you today?" asked the guy in the black speedo.

"Weird. It's been weird."

"Splendid!" said the man in the tankini.

"O-Ok." Said Kilroy.

"We were discussing a bit of serendipity of events regarding our scheduled portrait and your eventful proximity. Would you like to be in the picture?" he asked.

"Bully!" said the one in the Victorian suit.

"Sorry to be so forward." Said the one in the speedo while he looked admonishingly at his companions.

"I guess." Said Kilroy, realizing she'd never catch up with the... whatever it was.

She followed them to the end of the street. She saw what looked a lot like the White House sitting at the head of the T-intersection. She also saw a man with

31

strange hair carrying a digital projector into a black velvet tent.

"Ah yes. Before Antebellum America. The Presidential Mansion. It was burned down in 1814 by British forces. Retaliation over our attack on York, Ontario. The war of 1812. The casus belli being some damnable business of impressment. And the blockade! A malicious flouting of International Maritime Law! The Napoleonic wars. Also, a bit of outrage over a skirmish at sea between the USS President and the HMS Little Belt. Their stratagem to arm the Indians gave us a fuck of a time. In 1813 we defeated the Tecumseh Confederacy on Lake Erie. We won—the British won. Everybody won. Except for the Indians. Damnable business, that." Mansplained the man in the Victorian swimsuit. As he spoke, he aged decades before her eyes. Older, he looked familiar.

Suddenly, the Presidential Mansion burst into flames.

The one in the tankini approached, and he also was

transformed from young to old. She recognized him too and was non-plussed.

"What matter are you boring her with?" asked Benjamin Franklin in his blue tankini.

"Swerve." Said Kilroy as she scowled. She pivoted and walked away.

Kilroy approached the man with the strange hair. He was wearing dramatic eye make-up and had a contoured face. His nose glowed from beneath his sheer coverage. He was painting the flames of the Presidential Mansion.

"Hey, is your name Andy Warhol?" asked Kilroy.

"Indeed it is." He replied.

"Wow. I read about you in school."

"Ah. What school?"

"East Madison High."

"Oh. I thought you meant college."

"Nah. I'm a soldier."

"Do you have plans to go to college after?"

"I don't know yet. I'm focusing on getting back for now."

"As you should. May I take your picture so I can make your stencils?"

"Sure. Stencils?"

"Are you familiar with the work of Banksy?"

"I've heard of him. Isn't he a graffiti artist?"

"Precisely. He can recreate any of his work as I did. My studio was my factory. I used screen printing. Banksy's studio is everywhere. He uses stencils. I've married his technique with my own. I have a portable factory in which I produce stencils on the spot." Said Warhol as he gestured to the black velvet tent next to him.

"You make stencils with pictures?"

"Yes. I trace from the projected image. Will you please take off your mask for a moment?"

She took a deep breath and then held it as she grabbed the nose of her mask and pulled it up and off. She smelled the burning mansion. Warhol began snapping shots of her with a digital camera.

"Walk away a bit so I can get more of you in." he asked. She took a few steps away and let him get a few more shots before she exhaled and pulled her mask back down.

"Got what you needed?" she asked.

"I do. You look very exotic, if I may say."

"Don't." she replied. She looked down at her phone and unlocked it.

The phone came to life. She watched as the phone's living user navigated to Facebook. Kilroy learned that her name was Emilie Brooke Houston.

"Sunday Funday! Binge-watching Gossip Girl. This show was the shit in middle school! Remember all those slumber parties? @MadelineWertz @Valerie-Stephens"

Kilroy looked at the date and time. It was November 18th, 2018. 11:07 p.m. She looked up at Warhol as "Fire, Water, Burn" by The Bloodhound Gang began to play. She saw the one in the black speedo age from young to mid 40's. She recognized him as John F. Kennedy. He stood looking at her with arms akimbo, nodding.

"Sup." Kilroy said.

"Not a lot." Shrugged Kennedy.

"Hold up." Said Kilroy as she walked over to a single sweat sock that had fallen to the ground. She smelled that it was clean and put it in her pocket.

"Looking for an excuse not to talk to me?" asked

Kennedy.

"No. I needed that sock." Said Kilroy unconvincingly. She had yet to find any menstrual products for sale. She remembered how a girl she sat by in High School said she used an inside-out sweat sock as a pad when her family couldn't afford pads and tampons for her.

"You needed one sock?"

"Yeah. Look, my… uh. Fuck it. I have periods, man. Mind your business."

"Enough said." Replied Kennedy.

"So…" Kilroy began awkwardly.

"What branch are you?" asked Kennedy.

"Army. Corporal." She said. She realized she wasn't wearing her jacket, so he couldn't see her rank.

"I tried the army. Was medically disqualified. Got into the Naval reserve and saw some action there. Wold War 2."

"Pacific theatre?"

"Yes. So, Benjamin says you don't like him. May I ask why?"

"Because he owned slaves!"

"Oh. Right. I'm pretty sure all of that is behind him. He really wants you to like him. Think you could just talk to him for a second? Give him a chance."

"A chance. How about I take this chance to give him a piece of my mind."

"As you wish." Said Kennedy. Kilroy walked away over to Benjamin. Kennedy watched them just out of earshot.

"So, that portrait of me. " Kennedy said to Warhol.

"What about it?"

"Why?"

"Why not? Your death made you huge! A pop-art

martyr."

"I still can't get my head around what I am to people."

"Death is wasted on the dead." Said Warhol as "Peaches" by The Presidents of the United States of America played. He began to photograph Kennedy. They paused and looked over at Franklin and Kilroy as she raised her voice.

"I liked that one of my wife." Kennedy awkwardly filled in.

"I do too. I wouldn't paint something I didn't like."

Kennedy watched as Kilroy and Franklin walked back over to join them.

"Teddy?" called Warhol to the man in the Victorian swimsuit. He walked over to stand for pictures.

"So, Roosevelt. Who all is going to be at this pool party we're going to?" asked Franklin.

"The guest list is extensively intellectual. It will be quite stimulating."

"Intellectual isn't the stimulation I was hoping for. Will there be babes?" he asked.

Kilroy pulled her phone out, tired of this conversation and drained from the intense discussion she'd just had. She began snooping on Houston's Facebook for memes. She saw a posted cartoon featuring Jason from the "Friday the 13th" franchise. Her post was about all of her classes moving online. She looked at the date. It was March 13th, 2020.

"Hey, hey guys!" she said, frantic.

"What's the trouble?" replied Franklin.

"How exactly does time work, like… time here compared to time in the living world."

"That's hard to pin, exactly. The time streams have little to do with one another. Information travels between the worlds based on the memory of that object, be it a newspaper stand, a phone, a television, whatever. What time the object projects from it's life of usage is random. The information is scrambled."

"So time didn't just advance, like, 2 years in the living world." She said as she held up her phone. Franklin viewed the date.

"Certainly not. Granted, it's impossible to know how time is passing in the living world in relation to your time here. You may return the instant you disappeared. You may return much later with everyone you once knew gone."

"I just find out when I get back."

"Precisely."

"Pepper" by Butthole Surfers started to play.

"Time is an illusion and a cruel joke." Interjected Warhol as he emerged from his tent with stencils and paint. He sorted the paint into two color groups: one set of colors for the dead presidents and founding father and a second much brighter palate for Kilroy.

"So, have you secured suitable lodging for yourself?" asked Roosevelt.

"Yeah. I live on the Titanic doing Human Excavation."

"Bully!" he exclaimed.

"I remember being infatuated with the sea as a lad. Then I spent a fair bit rowing boats. My thirst was sated. I recall one night of grueling travel in which one of my compatriots, one Collins, was pissed to the brink and refused to row. I yeeted him into the river. Each time he tried to reboard, we would row hence out of reach and ask, 'Will you row?'. The wanker would refuse each time. We made fair sport of this until he agreed. He was a sour companion hence. After we reached our destination, he split. I never saw him again after spending a fair bit on him. Kept him with drink. He was a riot to drink with but an all-around bastard." Told Franklin.

"I have some experience with boats. Our PT was blown in half. I gathered 10 survivors, and we swam to Plum Pudding Island. I pulled Pappy MacMahon by a strap on his life jacket gripped in my teeth. There was no food. No water. We swam to an island called Olansana, I learned. Coconuts but nothing else. George Ross and I swam a bit to yet another island. Came back in a canoe we found with some crackers and candy. There was water too. We must've been a sight coming back. Never been that happy about a piece of shit boat."

"Handlebars" by Flobots filtered through.

"A boat in the right place is a boon indeed. It was 1886 on the ranch. The Little Missouri was iced over from winter, and as the ice broke up. It moved slowly, creating walls that creamed over like breakers upon the shore." Droned Roosevelt.

Kilroy was spacing off while he told his tedious story about the citizen's arrest of some boat thieves. She unlocked her phone again.

The date said October 23rd, 2018. She watched as Snapchat came to life. The phone's user filled the screen as she scrolled through different filters. She was beautiful. She saw that the screen name contained her middle and last name.

"So, Brooke." Kilroy said to herself.

She touched the screen to see what happens. She saw the navigation buttons appear. She went to the home screen and clicked on the gallery. She went to the gallery and looked at the folders. She found one labeled "No". She opened it.

The folder was full of pictures of beautiful, thin women. Their heads weren't pictured. Some were in underwear. A few were nude. Most were clothed. There were hundreds of these pictures. She scrolled through and found, interspersed among the women were pictures of a sad Houston looking in the mirror in her underwear.

"Lady and gentlemen." Signaled Warhol. They all looked toward the finished portrait. "Sabotage" by The Beastie Boys started up.

She saw that the men were painted as their older, famous selves. They were depicted from the knees up. Kilroy was shown holding her mask with her gun on her shoulder. Her head was down, looking at her phone.

The others were each looking in a different direction. Roosevelt had a wistful expression. Kennedy had a 1000-yard stare. Franklin was standing with his hands on the straps of his bright blue tankini, like suspenders. He looked smug. The Presidential Mansion burned behind them.

"I present to you: "Four Jackasses"." Announced Warhol.

CASSETTE ROULETTE

Kilroy got off the train at a Copenhagen station. She followed her nose to the Starbucks.

"Has the chocolate sauce appeared yet?" yelled the Barista to the back.

"WHAT!" the back-of-house man yelled back. All he could hear was the sound of espresso machines and customers. This place was getting slammed in the world of the living. Front-of-house was getting far less noise.

"I said has the chocolate sauce appeared yet?"

"Yeah, you can have a beer!"

"No! Chocolate sauce! I'm going back there. Gimme just a minu-" said the Barista as she looked at Kilroy and did a double-take. She shook her head and headed to the back.

Kilroy pulled her phone out. The screen came to life. She watched it unlock as Houston navigated to Snapchat. She scrolled through filters. From the background, Kilroy could see that she was on some kind of train. The date said March 24th, 2019. It was 02:36.

"Atlanta airport, amirite? I'm back! I miss spring break already! It was good to see Abuela and Papi and all my cousins, too!"

Kilroy put the phone back in her pocket when the Barista came up with a big thing of chocolate sauce.

"How may I help you?" she asked.

"A café mocha? Large."

"Right on." She said as she got to work.

Kilroy got her phone back out of her pocket and opened YouTube. She scrolled through some 'Witcher 3' gameplay videos. The phone came to life.

Houston navigated to Instagram and took a picture of her made bed. It was 05:40. The date was April 1st, 2019.

"Back to 5 am wake-up time! My bed is ready for tonight, and I will be stoked to see it." She wrote. Kilroy noticed that she used the international time format.

"Mars?" called the Barista. Kilroy collected her coffee and left.

She sauntered, admiring the deep brown woodwork of this vintage train station. She stepped outside to find Night-break fast approaching. She walked straight down a narrow lane.

Night-break hit as she saw the woman sitting by a vardo. Her tattoos glowed. Her arms and chest were covered. She wore a corset and a pair of ripped jeans with biker boots. The woman got up and waved her over.

"Hey! C'mere." She said.

Kilroy paused and considered ignoring her, but she was curious. She walked over.

"What's up?" asked Kilroy.

"It's what's up with you! Have a seat." She said as she gestured to one of two hunter green plastic lawn chairs.

Kilroy sat down. She was surrounded by candles and oil lamps. Fairy lights hung from the top of the vardo out to tiki torches stuck in the ground. The golden firelight contrasted with the blue moon and led lights.

"Nice place."

"Thanks. Mind pressing play on the tape player, dear?"

Kilroy pressed play. "Darkness" by Lord Byron filled the spaces. They listened as "In the Beginning" by the Statler Brothers played, followed by a sound clip from "The Ref" about shutting the fuck up for 10 seconds. Then "Friends of P" by The Rentals started to play.

"What's your name?" asked the tattooed woman.

"Kilroy." She said as she set her gun next to her.

"And your first name?"

"There's two of them. Lucretia Valentina. But I go by Mars."

"Ok, Mars. Family name?"

"Sort of. My mother's middle name is Jupiter."

"I see. Well, my name is Maud. Maud Wagner. I waved you over to offer you a tattoo. Would you be interested?"

"For real?"

"Yes. Totally free of charge. I want to ink something that's going to stay. I'm tired of dead skin." She said as she lit a joint. She undid and redid her top bun with the joint in her mouth.

"Ok. Sure."

"What do you want?" asked Wagner as she handed Kilroy a little notebook and pen.

Kilroy thought hard. She was coming up blank.

"Hey, what's your birthday?" asked Wagner as she pulled out an iPad.

"March 21st."

"Aries. What year and time?"

"1998. And 02 hundred and 3."

"Oh wow! Mars was in Aries when you were born!" said Wagner as she showed Kilroy her astrological birth chart.

"What does that mean?"

"Maybe you could do an Aries symbol inside a Mars symbol. It doesn't mean anything. It's just neat because of your name and sign."

Kilroy looked down at the paper. She'd been doodling

hearts. She looked at the most perfect one and carefully drew an Aries symbol inside of it. She liked how it looked like a happy owl face.

Jim Carrey's voice came on after the song. It was from when he played the Riddler. He talked about a small box on people's TVs that gave him all of their information. Then he belched the word "I."

"This is what I want. In red. Here." Said Kilroy as she handed Wagner the notebook and rolled up her shirt to expose her shoulder.

"Alright," Wagner said as she began to wash and shave the area. A remix of David Bowie's "Man Who Sold the World" played. She poured some Smirnoff on a cloth and wiped Kilroy's shoulder. She then took a drink and offered Kilroy the bottle. Kilroy lifted her mask to drink. Maud watched her and got a look at her face.

A strange sound clip describing a torture dream played. Then "Tortoise" by God Lives Underwater began. Kilroy looked around; the vardo had 4 huge spoke wheels fitted with modern tires. It was painted green and had a curved roof. There was a round window in the small Dutch door.

The lawn chairs were on either side of the petite stairs. There were two folding tables set up in a V shape. On them were display cases and metal grids for hanging hooks to display goods on. She'd seen them in shady mall stores and outdoor sales.

A creepy sound clip from the same movie as the torture dream played. In it, a young woman says she wants to suffer like a child. Then "My Friends" by Red Hot Chili Peppers played.

Kilroy could see lots of Kiss nail sets in the nearest display case, both glue on and imPress. There was also a set of clippers in a sleek metal case.

Next to it was a grid with T-shirts hanging. One she recognized as from Strange Music. There was also a Nirvana T-shirt, a Happy Noodle Boy shirt, Five Finger Death Punch, Marilyn Manson, The Doors, Bob Marley,

A tie-dye shirt with a big green marijuana leaf, and a very neon fanny pack.

A sound clip from "The Crying Game" played. It was a man asking another about what he knows of his own nature. Then "You" by REM played.

On the other side, by Wagner, was a rotating case of sunglasses. Next to that, on the table, were several clear cases full of jewelry. There were nose rings, belly button jewelry, a variety of gauge plugs, eyebrow bars, spiked collars and wristbands, a pewter bat necklace, a coffin choker, a coffin locket, a coffin coin purse, coffin earrings, several skull rings, a Claddagh ring, a spider ring, glow in the dark bangles, a wrist band with skulls and pirate swords, a plain black wristband, and some cherry clip-on earrings.

Next to that was a display of posters. Some were blacklight reactive. There was a blacklight on them. The only ones that weren't UV reactive were a black and tye-dye tapestry with mushrooms and a Banksy poster.

It was "Grin Reaper."

"So, what's the deal with this tape that's playing?" asked Kilroy.

"I got them as a set with the tape player. There are 36 in total. They return to their cases and, uh, the case for the cases. You can take a look. The tapes are on the shelf of the table under the player." "Vow" by Garbage played.

Kilroy picked up the cassette holder and looked at the multi-colored spines of the cases. She picked up the empty case by the player, which she saw was also a radio alarm clock. It had an open mouth with ruby lips on the front. The word "shriek" was inside the mouth. Under the mouth and to the right of it were two rats. One green. One pink. There was an alarmed eye just below black drips. It was pixelated.

She opened the case and took out the insert. Inside she saw a giant eye with jagged lashes and the rest of the green rat. She folded it open and found it was a collage on a blank recordable cassette tape insert. The songs were listed inside, but not the sound clips. She saw that "Vow" was mislabeled as "Stupid Girl."

A clip from "The Ref" about a big wooden cross played. Then a Nine Inch Nail song played for a minute and was scrambled. She was startled and looked at the tape player. The scrambling stopped, and the following clip played. It was from that creepy movie again. Wagner laughed at her.

"So, who were you, Maud?" asked Kilroy. "Stutter" by Elastica played.

"Did you ever want to run away and join the circus as a kid?" she asked.

"No."

"That's what I did. I was a contortionist, and I did air stunts. I had to be fearless night after night. A bored crowd is a lucrative opportunity. I got myself some lessons in tattooing to maximize my earning power. The circus is a circus inside and out, and I knew I didn't want to be there forever."

"When did you get tatted?" asked Kilroy.

"Which time? I got these tattoos poked into me like I'm doing to you right now. It was over some time. Many sessions." Wagner lit another joint and passed it to Kilroy.

"Word." Said Kilroy as she lifted her mask to take a hit from the offered doobie. She pulled her mask back down and exhaled into the space between her face and the HEPA tamp on in the nose. Hotboxed. She passed it back to Wagner.

Another clip from that creepy movie played, followed by a weird high voice describing a vague and exploitive situation. Then "Backsliders" by The Toadies played.

"I taught my daughter, Loretta, to tattoo so she'd always have something to fall back on. It's like sewing in a way. Machine tattoos were taking over. We were of a dying art, and I didn't want to see it be that way." A clip about liars from that creepy movie played. Then "Numb" by U2 began.

"I've known a few people who have gotten tattoos hand done like this. It's coming back, so maybe it worked." Replied Kilroy.

"So how about you? What was home to you?"

"My mother and I lived at home with my grandparents. We took care of my Grandpa. He had severe memory issues and needed constant supervision. He only half knew who my mother and I were, but his face lit up each time Grandma explained about us being his daughter and granddaughter. I know he loved us.

"Mom worked plant work right out of high school. She married my Dad, but then they got divorced shortly after we all moved in with Grandma to help." Said Kilroy as she absentmindedly ran her thumb along her startlingly long nails.

She looked out to the lane and saw a baby with a glowing marble pattern crawl by. There were at least five cats visible from where she sat.

A sound clip about never parting and always in the heart played in a jagged and looping fashion. This was followed by a loop of breaking glass. Then "Say it ain't so" by Weezer played.

They silently listened as the song played through. It was followed by yet another clip from that creepy churchy movie.

"Do you know what movie those are from?" asked Kilroy.

"I haven't a clue."

A voicemail of a man saying "God bless you" to a guy named Shawn played. Then was a loop of someone talking about being hard to resist. Then the man said "God bless you" again. This was followed by Latin chanting and some sped-up audio. Then the tape clicked to a stop.

"Want me to turn it over?"

"Either that or choose a new tape. Cassette Roulette."

"Eh." She said, feeling she couldn't choose a tape without moving too much. She flipped the tape over. Wagner paused her tattooing to take a drink of the vodka. She handed Kilroy the bottle. She sipped it under her mask.

A woman ordering food at a fast-food restaurant played. Then the man at the register called her a whore, and she started cussing loudly. It startled them.

"Destination Unknown" by The Replicants played. Kilroy could see fireworks going off in the distance as the nightly partying went into full swing. She'd been warned about this.

She was startled again by more cussing from the tape.

"Are you ok?" asked Wagner. "Tomorrow" by Silverchair began.

"Yeah. I was just spacing off, thinking about my Dad's books."

"He writes?"

"He did. He's dead now. Cancer. He was a cop before, but he retired early to write these books. I read the first chapter of the first one. It followed a guy who finds a little Grey alien in his shed holding a kilo of cocaine. Then the little dude goes "Gang, gang," and he runs off." The story of the scorpion and the frog from "The Crying Game played. Then they listened to "One of Us" by Joan Osborne.

"Been a minute since I heard this song." Said Wagner.

"What if God rolled cannabis." Said Kilroy. Wagner smiled and handed her an unlit blunt and a lighter.

"I'll let your start this one-off."

A strange parking lot rape poem played. Kilroy lifted an eyebrow. "Where Boys Fear to Tread" by The Smashing Pumpkins rocked out. Kilroy took her phone out of her pocket to check the time and then caught herself. She laughed.

"What is time, even?" she said.

"Got somewhere to be?" asked Wagner.

"Nah. I'm off. I do human excavation—night-break crew. Normally I'd be suiting up right about now, but it's day 9 of the cycle. We work 8 days a week. We rest on the 9th. The Titanic doesn't sail today."

"Ah. Well, it's a small tattoo, so I'm almost done." She said as she accepted the blunt from Kilroy.

Kilroy turned her phone on. She watched as Houston uploaded her application to graduate. The date was December 7th, 2019. It was 12:24.

She hopped on Facebook and began a post about her own self-reflection. She added pictures from the pancake feed in her neighborhood. She talked about how her current living situation was different from the dorms and how evanescent it all was. A looping clip from an interview asking a man if he uses drugs to deal with the pain of what he writes about played.

Kilroy scrolled through Brooke's timeline, and "Planet Telex" by Radiohead played. She saw all kinds of anti-Trump memes and Black Lives Matter posts. Kilroy smiled at this. She was really starting to like Houston.

"So, Brooke, can I use the phone now?"

"What was that?" asked Wagner.

"Nothing, Maud. Just talking to this phone lady."

"Ah. Be careful you don't get too wrapped up in her life." Warned Wagner. A clip from Clockwork Orange played in which Alex finds out he's killed his latest victim. Then "Guilty" by Gravity Kills played.

Kilroy turned the screen off and on. She put in the

lock pattern and opened Facebook. She saw the latest post on her timeline.

"I've been looking forward to this class since Freshman year! Abnormal Psychology, here I come!" it said. Next to it was a selfie from Snapchat with cat ears and eyes. The day was August 27th, 2019.

Some random noise played, followed by "Speaking of Happiness" by Gloria Lynne. Kilroy turned the phone screen on and off again. She saw Houston rapidly open the lock and open messenger. She messaged her friend named Gloria. It was February 8th, 2019, at 07:42 am.

"OMG bitch. Fucking men!"

"What happened?"

"Some asshat just insulted me and called me a basic bitch when I turned him down at the gym."

"WTF!!"

"He asked if I was DTF, and I was like NTFN. No the

fuck Not."

"Lol. I'm totally stealing that."

Kilroy admired how early both Houston and her friends were awake. A clip from "Charlie and the Chocolate Factory" featuring Veruca Salt played, followed by "Forsythia" by Veruca Salt, the band.

Houston navigated over to Snapchat and took a selfie outside of the school gym. The morning light was very flattering.

"Ok, and I'm done." Said Wagner. She wiped it again with the vodka.

"Dope. Thanks. Hey, can I buy a few things?"

"Sure, what did you have in mind?" said Wagner. She took a spiked leather wristband out of the case and handed it to Kilroy, who accepted it.

Kilroy pointed to the case full of nails. Wagner unlocked it.

"I'd like those clippers and those nails. No. Yeah. The black ones. And that Banksy poster, too. Also, is that a sleep set?" she asked, pointing to a hanger with a black tank top and pair of shorts hanging from it. The set was covered in red anarchy symbols.

"You got it." She said. She handed her the clippers, nails, tank, and shorts set and rolled up the poster. Kilroy gave her 40 euros.

"It was great meeting you. Thank you for the tattoo."

"Is it your first?"

"Yeah."

"I'm delighted! Now get outta here and enjoy your night off."

THE COLD

Kilroy looked over Necropolis at night. It was lit exquisitely. She was smoking a Djarum Black clove cigarette. The spikes of her wristband clinked against the rail. She'd trimmed her nails and had on the black imPress nails. Her jacket was in her room with her gun, and her mask was hanging from her elbow.

"Bela Lugosi's Dead" by Bauhaus played from her phone. Heavy activity from the phone's user seemed to come in waves. There were long periods when Houston's use didn't interfere with Kilroy's use.

"Why the glum song?" asked Manny.

"Because Bela Lugosi IS dead, and you're going to hear about it, Brenda." Joked Kilroy.

"Whatever you're smoking smells good, by the way."

Answered Manny as he made his way to the Marconi room.

Kilroy lingered until a breeze told her about herself. She lifted an arm and smelled her pits. She went to her room to drop off her pants, mask, and gun. She retrieved her new toiletries and towel. She saw the new pajamas on a chair. She'd forgotten about them. She felt a jolt of joy as she grabbed them and headed to the pool room.

She checked the plumbing to see that everything was still connected. She'd had to help solder once already. Everything looked good. She undressed and turned the water on. She set her stuff up on the shelf next to everyone else's.

She didn't want to overwork her hair, so she did the two shampoos and conditioner to start with. She lathered twice as the huge tub filled and used the shower head to rinse.

She put in the conditioner as the water reached

the top. She shut it off and soaked for a bit. Then she opened her new soap and washcloths. The washcloths were red, and there was Korean writing on the package. The soap was a patchouli-scented bar made from goat milk. She also had a little bamboo soap saver to set it on.

She wet the cloth and lathered twice, scrubbing hard. Then she rinsed and soaked, watching the reflected light from the pool water on the ceiling. It was her own private patchouli-scented hell, she realized. The cloying darkness ate at her in the silence, leaving her soul cold in the hot bath.

Then she snapped out of it. She washed her vulva and ass crack with her hands, washed her hands, rinsed out her conditioner, standing with her head upside down and the showerhead close as she worked through with her hands, and got out. She toweled off with a waffle textured towel. It was pink with black trim. She wondered who had it in the Land of the Living and what they'd think about her using it.

She got in her pajamas. She loved them. She'd always had a flat stomach, being a dancer and an athlete and, lately, a soldier. Her friends told her she was lucky she could wear whatever she wanted. Secretly she envied their tummies. Kilroy always liked pooch on women. She'd figured out long ago that she was not her own type.

She got her clothes and boots together in a bundle with her towel over her shoulders and headed out. She was halfway to the Grand Staircase when Da Vinci caught up with her. She could smell the pine tar soap on him.

"So you're the one using the Turkish Baths." She observed.

"Guilty as charged. How did you surmise that?"

"Smell. I used your soap the first day I was here. It was weird. I brushed my teeth with it. So why don't you use the tub with everyone else?"

"Bathing was a different thing for me in life. The Turkish Baths have their upsides. A hot room for the cold water. Privacy. A bench."

"Alright." Said Kilroy with oblivious misunderstanding.

"There was something I wanted to speak to you on, in fact. I have for you an opportunity to do some good and gain some profit. Would you be interested in a mission?"

"What's the mission?"

"I've tracked a sadist who preys on children and found his latest hiding place. We are going to dispatch him for once and for all. We will put him in a barrel, weld it shut, and kick him into the ocean on the other side of the sphere with all the wildlife. We will fly there. There's an altitude cap. We can only fly so high. And we must stay within temperature thresholds for the plane to work right, so we must fly in a spiral, following the Break-line. We will fly in front of it, beginning at night.

As we circle out, the Break-line's velocity will overtake us, and we will arrive at the volcanic rim during the day. After which temperature is controlled by the respective climates, and we can fly straight onto the ocean."

"Hold up. You have planes and shit? Can you fly me to the Zig?"

"I'm sorry, but the best I can do is pay you for work. I'm rich, but I'm not so rich I can afford to give too much away. I'm invested in restructuring the whole city after your arrival partially dismantled it. I pay a lot of people, a lot of people. I'm sorry. I can afford to fly to depose a criminal who is torturing and eating children over and over again. I cannot afford to fly a soldier capable of going herself."

"Is there any way you'd help a killer go home?"

"I've helped two. One was Albert Fish, the man we are going to take care of. He came here and found it to be a sort of sadistic paradise. The victims never expire. The game is never over. Some killers enjoy turning people into things. Fish simply gives a shit about the pain. He also mutilates himself so he can enjoy it in his victims more."

"Who was the other one?"

"The other killer was 9 years old. Her name was Nikki. She'd killed her mother's rapist."

"Oh."

"Indeed."

There was an awkward silence.

"So, what determines who spawns in Necropolis and who spawns in the sands?"

"I have yet to ascertain that answer. All I know is where you die is where you go."

"So, like those Russian cosmonauts who died out in space would..."

"Where you die is where you go." Interrupted Da

Vinci, holding up one finger.

"Ok. I get what you mean."

"I'm not sure that you do. Tell me, how well do you wash yourself?"

"Pretty well. I shampoo twice, soap twice, wash my hands after I wash my ass."

"Why?"

"Because they have just been in my booty crack. I feel like I need to wash them."

"For how long?"

"Pardon?"

"How long do you wash your hands?"

"Not that long. Like the normal amount? I don't understand where you're going with this."

Da Vinci paused, considering telling her something. She saw in his face when he came to a decision.

"Good night, Mars." He said as he walked away.

Kilroy was confused. She headed to the Breakfast Saloon. Inside, she picked up an éclair. As she ate, she sensed someone behind her. She turned around and saw a tiny woman. It was the woman she saw being taken out of her tank on her first day of work.

"Helo." She mouthed softly, her voice blunt.

"Hello." Responded Kilroy.

"Where's Kilroy?" she asked.

"I'm right here." Responded Kilroy.

The woman shook her head and pointed to her face, outlining a long nose with her hand.

"Oh. My mask. That's a plague mask. I'm Kilroy. Kilroy is me. Mars Kilroy."

"Ok. Mars Kilroy. What am I?" she asked, pointing to herself.

"I'm sorry, I don't know you."

The woman looked frustrated. Kilroy looked around the vast dining hall to see a few rescued souls conspicuously minding their own business over their food. She looked back to the folding tables containing the perpetual feast. She looked back at the woman.

"Calm down. What are you trying to tell me?"

"Mars." She pointed to Kilroy. "Me. What is my Mars?"

"Oh, name! You want a name. Ok holy shit. That's a lot of pressure. Let me think."

"Yes. Name!"

"Uhm, how about Lillith?" reached Kilroy, looking for a cool biblical name.

"Lil-ith. I am Lillith."

"So, I'm glad we got that ironed out. I'm going to go now." Said Kilroy, feeling uncomfortable as she grabbed two more pastries and a can of seltzer water.

She went out the door and ran up to her room before anyone else could see her. The ship's cat, Tugboat, was sleeping on her bed. He was a real motherfucker of a cat. He had long ginger hair and chased most other cats off the ship. He didn't take any shit and had a General of a great war's countenance and bearing.

She set her snacks on a small table and picked up her phone. It wasn't long before her phone came to life.

Houston opened up messenger. It was October 1st, 2019, 16:10.

"Hi mom!"

"Hey sweetie! How are you?"

"I'm good. Pretty normal day, except I got a bizarre call from my own number, though. There was a lot of interference, and the voice on the other end was frantically telling me I die in hurricane Katrina at Piggly Wiggly."

"Be careful! Don't answer your phone if it happens again! There are things out there that you don't know about that can hurt you!"

"Don't worry, Mom. I'm in a really safe place!"

"How is the renting situation going in Pine Lake?"

"It's stellar! This house is so cute, and my room is totes cottage core. This neighborhood had its own police and a lake."

"Sounds lovely! I hope I can visit you for Thanksgiving and see!"

"There's a pancake feed one Saturday of every month. And everyone is really nice. A little lacking in boundaries. This old hippie lady poked her head in my room just to get a look at me and my space. I did not know how to react, really."

Houston navigated away from messenger and opened Tumblr. She looked at her messages and saw:

"Hey, sorry but I really need someone to talk to." From Deteriorating-Dumbo. Houston opened it. Her username was "Stick-Witch".

"What's up?" she asked.

"My mom. She made me feel really bad after a binge. She doesn't want me to be anorexic, but she also doesn't want me to be fat. The hypocisy is enough to make me want to kill myself."

"Are you seriously considering suicide? Like, do you have a plan?"

"*hypocrisy. And no. Not that far yet. It's just a feeling of wanting to escape."

"I'm glad you aren't planning to end yourself. Have you been self-harming?"

"I gave myself an eraser burn in class on Thurs but otherwise, no."

"Why'd you do that?"

"I was bored."

Then, a chat bubble from her mother popped up. She opened it.

"Do you need to maybe install a lock on your door?"

"Maybe. I'll ask about it." She said. She navigated back to her conversation with Deteriorating-Dumbo. "Why did you really do it?"

"There's these girls. They're really pretty, and everyone treats them like they deserve the world, and they treat my friends and me like total shit. Maybe if I looked more like them, I could somehow be better than them, and then I could feel alright."

"Honey. There's no ceiling. There's no top of the ladder or level you can reach where you're finally content. The benchmark will always move. There will always be women you hate yourself over. There are people out there who make those girls look like bullshit."

"God that just makes me feel so much worse."

"That's why you have to learn to accept yourself as you are. You can work on yourself and compare where you were to where you are, but never compare someone's outside life to your inner world."

"I wish it was that simple,"

Brooke opened her mother's chat bubble.

"So, how are all your plants in my room?"

Kilroy closed the phone. She felt whiplash from Houston's double life.

"So, Brooke. You're anorexic. Not a lesbian."

Kilroy looked at her "Grin Reaper" poster on the wall as she ate her apple fritter. She opened the phone back up. She opened YouTube and typed a Lupe Fiasco song in the search bar. Suddenly messenger popped open. It was November 28th, 2018, at 18:34.

"OMG, Glory! I am so not ready for this gadget flow."

"Wtf?"

"*Finals. Fucking auto predict. So random lol"

"Nope!" exclaimed Kilroy.

Kilroy turned the phone off and threw it on the bed next to Tugboat.

SHELLEY - 2018

Shelley didn't know she was autistic. She only knew her senses were overloaded. It was all she could do to bear it. The heroin helped. A lot. Her clothes no longer irritated her. Things could be as obnoxious as hell, and it wouldn't touch her.

They don't call it a fix for nothing, but it was a slippery horse to catch. Money became Monopoly money. She thought of every stack in terms of grams, white and clean to black and oily. It didn't matter as long as she could shoot it.

Shelley had been walking since 03:00 that morning. She was beginning to have trouble breathing. She turned a corner and could see The Vortex in Little 5 Points, Atlanta, Georgia. She wanted to sit down. Her back muscles spasmed. She hadn't slept. Her anxiety was building, and she could feel increasing pressure within her body. Her pulse roared in her ears. She needed junk, bad.

Shelley was next to The Junkman's Daughter, an alternative book and clothing store. She remembered buying "Wall and Piece" by Banksy there. No one loved graffiti art like she did. Now she just wished the junk-man would come to be her daddy.

It was midmorning now, and people were around. She was filled with dread at the prospect of panhandling. She had severe issues looking people in the eye. She was ashamed of it. She drew up a measure of ragged strength and lifted her eyes from the sidewalk.

Just to the left of the massive spiral-eyes plaster skull that framed the Vortex restaurant entrance was a beautiful young woman. She was talking to a friend and holding her powder blue Hobo bag loosely behind her.

Shelley didn't know how she ran so quickly without passing out. Dots were floating in her vision, and everything sounded far away. She just hiked the stolen purse onto her shoulder as if it was hers. She wasn't stopping until she reached her dealer.

She turned up his back driveway and knocked on his back door softly. He took his time answering. He knew she wouldn't leave his stoop.

He opened the door and slowly reached for his fly in anticipation before noticing the stolen bag on her shoulder. He smiled.

15 minutes later, she was much steadier and loaded with a little white balloon and fresh needle and spoon. Now she just needed to deal with her soiled pants. There was a wet line up the seam of the ass of her jeans. She had an accident while walking.

Her aunt Kate lived close by in Cabbagetown. Shelley could borrow some clothes, shower, and maybe get her hair braided while she was still high, so it didn't feel like her aunt was trying to peel her head like an orange.

Shelley smiled as the Krog Street Tunnel came into view. She briefly felt worthy of the purse she carried. The slouchy blue thing was surprisingly comfortable on her shoulder.

This tunnel was one of her favorite places in the world. She'd begun her career as a graffiti artist when she was 15. She worked hard at it. She bought and studied books and tested different methods on different surfaces, all while dodging the cops. Her signature was a seashell. She didn't know it, but she was almost a King. That was before the heroin.

Beyond that magical bridge was Estoria. She was just minutes away from her aunt's house. She tried to think of a reason she needed new pants that had nothing to do with heroin. She was at the bottom of the long stairs up to her aunt Kate's porch. All she could think up was food poisoning.

She took a deep breath and climbed the stairs. She knocked. No answer. Nobody was home. She gazed at the Atlanta skyline from the porch.

She missed college. There were people there that gave a shit about what she had to say.

She walked around the house to the backyard and sat down on the back stoop. She pulled the stolen phone out of the purse and guessed the unlock pattern from the smears on the screen from a lovely brunch. It took 2 tries.

She started with music on YouTube, but she soon snooped through the social media accounts on the phone. She learned that the woman was named Emilie Brooke Houston. She was lovely.

Her YouTube feed was filled with videos with titles like "How to wake at 5 am", "5 Self-love Habits that Changed my Life", and "How to Read 100 Books in a Year." She watched a few and felt progressively worse about herself with each one.

She closed YouTube and opened Instagram. She

saw Brooke's pictures of her cottage core room, her meticulous planners and notes, her headless selfies in the body-length mirror, and her picture-perfect study space. She felt better when she realized these pictures might be stolen from other feeds.

The phone rang. The screen said the caller was "Mom". This shot Shelley through the heart. Her mother wasn't speaking to her right now. She shut the ringer off the phone and put it back in the purse. She saw her heroin kit among Houston's pretty things. There were two Mildliner highlighters with Japanese writing on them, a nice pen, a compact mirror, mascara, and tinted lip balm, her pocketbook, phone, and a small pink notebook.

Shelley picked up the notebook and opened it. It was the most beautiful planner she'd ever seen. She turned page after page of boxes, lists, journal entries, collections. There was even an index. She realized she recognized some of the spreads from Houston's Instagram.

Shelley's heart sunk. So, this woman really was that perfect. Tears streamed down her face. She felt deep within her that she could never be as organized, picturesque, productive, interesting, or charming as this woman in this phone.

She put the book back in the purse and pulled out her heroin. She gathered a little water from the hot tub next to her. Sepsis wasn't going to be a problem.

She shot the heroin. All of the ivory-colored heroin. It was 2 grams.

Kate came home to find her niece dead in her backyard. Her needle and spoon were next to her. She could smell the shit in her pants. She wished it was less tragic.

She touched her hair tenderly and remembered braiding it for her. Shelley had been a good girl. She was smart but strange, lonely, and shy. Nobody quite knew where things went wrong.

She picked up the pretty bag and opened it. She saw

16 missed calls from a stranger's mother. She went in-side and pulled out her own phone to call 911. She then hung Houston's pretty bag on the back of a kitchen chair and cried.

BY THE RIVER

Kilroy watched Lopez crack open another tall one. She was driving.

"Are you sure you should be drinking?" asked Kilroy.

"Who the fuck are we going to hit and kill?" asserted Lopez.

"If we crash, we could kill me."

"Would you rather drive?"

"If it would help, sure."

Lopez stopped the HumVee and got out. Kilroy climbed upfront as Lopez got in the back. They resumed their arc as Kilroy followed the local GPS network on an oldskool dash-mounted unit.

"Are you ok, Lisa?" asked Marley from the passenger seat. He'd been silently loading a bowl. He offered it to her, and she took a hit.

"Thanks. I got a lot on my mind. Someone got me fucked up, and instead of dealing with it, I decided not to deal with anything. I went to sleep. Now I'm fucked up over that. Dreams." She explained.

She passed the pipe to Kilroy.

"No thanks. I think one of us should be sober."

"That's a good idea, love." Chuckled Marley. His dreadlocks were tied back with a bandana, and he had a super large crochet hat over the top for warmth. It reminded Kilroy of Ali's turban.

They drove on for a while, the GPS repeating "Swerve left" and sometimes "Merge left" periodically until they heard "Your destination is on your right.

Kilroy heard Lopez open a packaged stopwatch. Packaged items can be used like new but usually need to be taken out of their packaging every time.

"Scheduled. Let's go make someone's night." said Lopez as she hit start.

"You're the foreman, Lisa." Said Marley.

"Bob is such a kiss ass." Lopez said to Kilroy with a smirk.

Kilroy got out of the HumVee and took off her mask. She gave the frigid air a sniff. She smelled blood and something musky. She followed the smell.

"Over here!" she yelled over the wind as she lit a flare. Marley walked over with a light kit. He stuck the tripods in the sand and used the light-diffusing umbrella-like attachment to shield the light socket from the sand as he screwed in the bulb. Then he turned them on.

Illuminated from 3 sides was a bloody arm jutting out from the sand. Near the arm was a moving poof of tawny fur.

Lopez arrived with the shovels and buckets. They got to work.

They unburied the human first, finding out that she was a woman. She had long dark hair and tanned skin.

"So we're digging up the dog?" asked Kilroy hopefully. Lopez and Marley looked at each other.

"You have to keep it under control." Said Lopez finally.

"Yes ma'am!" said Kilroy.

She began to dig around the tail. It was large and a little longer than that of a German shepherd. She found the hindquarters and started the free the legs. The legs began to kick. They were enormous.

"Hey…. Uh. Oh shit." Said Kilroy as she lifted one massive paw. The wind was helping unbury the creature.

Marley was watching with a furrowed brow. He

crawled into the small pit they'd created and used a pick to break up the sand on the side where it was highest. Kilroy saw the leg jerk when Marley accidentally hit the animal.

"Ja! How big is this thing?" he exclaimed. It was shaking itself out of the sand and into the small pit. It's skin was ragged and bare of most fur. Muscle and tendons were visible in places. It's haunches were much smaller than it's forelegs and shoulders. From its massive mouth jutted two long serrated teeth.

"No way." Said Kilroy as the saber tooth tiger looked her way. It got down on it's belly and crawled to her, whining. It was as if the creature was asking, 'can everything be beautiful again'. That's when Kilroy noticed the necklace around her great neck.

The smilodon reached her feet and butted her great head against Kilroy's knees. Kilroy looked at Lopez and Marley.

"Do we have room?"

"For it and the lady, but that's all. I'll drive." Said Marley. Lopez hit stop on the stopwatch and picked up the digging gear. She took the radio scanner off her belt and called up dispatch.

"Hey, Manny. You're not going to believe this shit." She was heard saying as she walked back to the HumVee.

Marley gave the woman they'd unburied a blanket and led her to the shotgun seat.

Kilroy faced the great cat, moving a little bit back each time it came toward her.

"Come on. That's a good boy. You're doing great." She coaxed with a soft voice. Soon, they were at the vehicle. Lopex had the back hatch open and was waiting inside with liniment warming in crockpots.

Kilroy climbed in, and the creature hopped in after her. It collapsed on it's side with it's head against Kilroy's hip. It began to suckle her coat like a kitten.

"We need to cover her wounds to keep her docile." Said Lopez as she handed her a warm pot of ointment.

Kilroy tested the temperature with one ungloved finger. She found it tolerable and scooped a handful to spread on the smilodon's shoulder.

Lopez was by the gnarled creature's feet. It was like a monster from a video game, and it was whining and making biscuits against the bundle of blankets by her massive paws.

Lopez turned on her flashlight on her phone and looked under the tail, finding that while it was hilariously small for the creature's body, it had protected the genitals.

"We have a She." Said Lopez.

"Ok."

"She's whining less."

"I think that's a good thing. What should we name

your, girl?"

The smilodon began making noises like a husky imitating human speech.

"Rah roh. Roh rah. Rah ror Rah."

"Talking girl. Sounds like she's saying Aurora." Said Lopez.

"Aurora." Kilroy spoke softly. The great cat purred.

"So you finally got your own stuff." Noted Lopez. Kilroy had been using her bathing supplies.

"Yes. And pajamas. I tried the showers in the room. That thing is bullshit. So's the tub. Like, you can bathe in a drinking fountain trickle of water or take a whole ass bath in some fart-smelling seawater."

"Yeah. That's what everyone said. Your nails look good."

"Thanks."

"Why'd you come here with so little, anyway?"

"I ditched my bag and load carrier so I could better maneuver."

"Hero shit. You're their corporal. Why?"

"I dunno. Guess I wanted a medal."

"You're gonna get your ass chewed on."

"Ugh. Yeah. It wasn't great. All I had in my pockets was some ammo, a compass, and a bunch of TP."

"You should get a sidearm while you're here." Observed Lopez.

"It couldn't hurt, I guess."

"Do you read?" Lopez asked out of the blue.

"Sometimes, I guess. Mostly for information. I never got into fiction. The only characters allowed to be normal human beings are white males. It's bullshit."

"That's a hot take. Want a beer?"

"Sure, I'll take one."

"This cooler is great. It's always full. The only problem is it's full of Pabst Blue Ribbon and Natty Light."

"My little goth heart was nursed to life with Pabst Bule Ribbon." Joked Kilroy. Lopez passed her one.

"Hey, you got a new phone too, right? Wanna see what's on that Spotify?"

"Okie-dokie." She said as the phone screen lit up. She unlocked it and went to Spotify. She searched through Houston's library and found a lo-fi station.

The music kept playing as she watched the screen come to life.

The date was September 9th, 2018. It was 10:27 on a Sunday. Kilroy watched her desk through the camera as Houston arranged everything just so. Then she took many shots. The notes on her desk were meticulous and very aesthetic. They were on African American psychology.

Kilroy watched as Houston navigated to Instagram to post her pictures for her many fans. Kilroy scrolled through her feed for a bit, admiring the DIY planner spreads. She learned that it was called Bullet Journaling, or Bujo.

She turned the screen off and absentmindedly pet Aurora's head. She was jerked awake by the HumVee slowing down and parking. She didn't even know she'd fallen asleep.

"Alright, you get a harness of some kind going. Here's a pile of Swedish harnesses and a baggie of carabiners."

Kilroy accepted the supplies and set about getting something around Aurora's shoulders. A Swedish harness is just a nylon loop. One can be made from rope. It took 6 of them to make a good harness for Aurora.

Kilroy coaxed the great cat out of the vehicle. Marley and Lopez headed up the scaffolding with the night crew supplies and light kit to avoid too much weight on those stairs.

It was treacherous for Kilroy to go up those stairs as she beckoned to Aurora. About halfway up, Aurora stalled. Then Da Vinci appeared and took the lid off of a great pot. He'd prepared a roast for this new guest.

The smell of cooking meat enticed Aurora, and she carefully and quickly negotiated the rickety scaffold stairs. On the top landing, she jumped onto the deck of the ship. Da Vinci wisely dumped the roast at her feet. She ate.

After her treat, Kilroy led her by the harness, following Da Vinci and Marley. They entered one of the lounges, and Kilroy saw a massive aquarium-like enclosure with gaskets. Attendants were pumping warmed liniment into it.

Da Vinci cautiously approached the smilodon. Kilroy stroked her head and cooed at her as Da Vinci examined her necklace.

"Sometimes the dead appear naked except for a sacred object they wore in life. I believe this was a Shaman's companion. As you can see, we are slightly equipped to deal with the prehistoric here. Simply guide her into the tank. I need to get back to work. Good luck!" said Da Vinci as he dipped out.

There were 4 large platforms by the tank's side; each one was 2 feet taller than the last. They served as great stairs. There was a steep grated ramp into the enclosure. Kilroy had some trouble getting her to go down the ramp. She wouldn't until the liniment was high enough for Aurora to try to walk on, then she stumbled in. She struggled for a second until the sheer relief overcame her.

Kilroy and Marley stayed until Aurora's eyes closed, and she fell into her first sleep in millennia.

"Want to smoke?" asked Marley.

"Sure. Writing room?"

"Let's go."

They left the lounge and walked the sort way to the reading and writing room. There was an entertainment center positioned in front of one of the couches. It had two TVs. One was a modern flat screen, and the other was a retro television from the early 90's. It was a Zenith, 30 pounds, and had an ass on it.

The modern TV was connected to a PS4. The old TV had a shelf full of retro game systems. There was a Super Nintendo, a Sega Genesis, an Atari, a Game Cube, an original Playstation, and a poor forgotten X-box. There were games on games.

Marley walked over to an ornate wooden box and removed a jar of Girl Scout Cookie. He put bottled water in a Graphix bong.

Kilroy turned on the TV and PS4. The menu music filled the spaces.

"Mute that!" snapped Marley.

"Sorry. What's the deal?" asked Kilroy as she muted it, a little annoyed.

"Every one of us here, except for you, has died. Many of us were conscious when we passed through the veil. It's a unique feeling. Dying is it's own emotion. It's a cold feeling. Like an Autumn in England under the fog, laying upon the peat, the wet soaking into you while light music plays. Music like the menu music."

"I felt that." Kilroy declared.

"No you didn't."

"I did. In fact, I feel it right now. This whole place has that mood. The fact that music sounds like death has me shook because I was just thinking how it fits this vibe I've felt since I got here."

"So the living feel the veil here. Interesting. Be sure to bring that up to Da Vinci." Advised Marley.

"Wanna load that bong? I could use a hit."

"Laughter helps, too. What year was it when you were in Syria?"

"2018."

"Want to see a show from the future?"

"Sure!"

"Go to Netflix. You're looking for a show called "Tiger King". It's slightly relevant to your status as a big cat mom."

Kilroy navigated to Netflix and started the first episode. Marley loaded the bong and passed her the green hit.

During a lull in the show and after a heavy dose of crazy from these tiger people, she pulled out her phone and turned it on.

The date was January 1st, 2019, at 10:02 in the morning. Houston navigated to Snapchat. She & her mother entered the frame, browsing the filters before settling on one that flattered them both. It was New Years Day brunch at a restaurant in Seattle. In the caption, she put that she was home for the holiday break and wanted to see as many people as possible before returning to Atlanta.

Houston navigated to FB and posted.

"New Year! Sorry for not wishing everyone a Happy 2019 last night! I was in FB jail! Someone called me a Becky, and I told them I was Cuban with fabulous Brazilian hair. Oops."

Kilroy put the phone away and watched the show. She noticed a theme.

"They talk about showing tigers off for money being exploitation, but they turn around and say they have to charge admission to feed the tigers. So, the tigers are paying their own rent and are kind of exploited like us."

"The tigers are indentured, you mean."

"Sort of. Yeah."

"Mars, you are at a disadvantage. You have to work to support your needs and your journey home. Here, the rest of us are free of need. We work for wants. We don't need our employers, but our employers need us. They bend over backward to please us."

"I noticed." Said Kilroy while she smoked the free weed provided by Da Vinci. She blew a cloud, remembering the sands and Clytemnestra drifting sideways on her four tracks at highway speeds.

"You know what my motto is ever since my Reggae days?"

"Don't worry, be happy?" joked Kilroy.

"McFerrin, one of these days. No. It was simply to trust Ja. Learn to trust when we can't understand. The eye of the Lord is upon you, even in this place. You were brought here for a purpose, and that purpose was to learn. Know that your choices here are your own. You could die here. That big cat of yours could be your protection or your demise. Remember that she loses her cool when you do. Choose trust. It's the same risk as choosing distrust."

"Alright. I won't worry. I'll be happy."

ABOUT THE AUTHOR

Anony Mou5

I am none of your business. I've come to fuck shit up. I'm the little engine that could, the wet twisted silk, the detonation's wind. I'm an animal: motherfuck this cage. Fuck up weights, books, and fuel  my brain. Play it loud. You choose your purpose.

Made in the USA
Middletown, DE
21 April 2021